A Bride For Noah

Book One

Brides of Broken Arrow

Cheryl Wright

A BRIDE FOR NOAH

Book One

Brides of Broken Arrow

Cover Artist: Black Widow Books

Editing: Amber Downey

Dedication

To Margaret Tanner, my very dear friend and fellow author, for her enduring encouragement and friendship.

To Alan, my husband of over forty-six years, who has been a relentless supporter of my writing and dreams for many years.

To Virginia McKevitt, cover artist and friend, who always creates the most amazing covers for my books.

To You, my wonderful readers, who encourage me to continue writing these stories. It is such a joy knowing so many of you enjoy reading my stories as much as I love writing them for you.

Table of Contents

Chapter One

Halliwell, Montana - 1880

"You can't be serious!" Noah Adams stood, his body shaking with fury. "Father gave me that land. You can't take it from me!"

Theodore Black sighed. "Do sit down, Noah, and let me finish reading the will. Everything will soon become clear."

Noah sat as directed, but still shook with rage. Barnabas Adams' entire estate had been bequeathed to his eldest son, Jacob, despite their deceased father's promise. He glanced across at Seth, who was two years younger than Noah at twenty-eight. He was far from happy.

"Jacob, as the oldest son, the main house is yours. You get all the property your father owned, depending on certain conditions."

Jacob would be thirty-two at his next birthday, and turned deathly white as the will was read. The way it looked now, Jacob would get everything. He'd always been more interested in the business side than working the land.

What on earth was their father thinking? And where did that leave both Noah and Seth? They'd each worked their allocated land for years, and were told, *guaranteed* it would legally be theirs when Father died. What was he playing at?

Theodore, or Teddy as everyone called him, glanced first at Noah, then Seth.

"Noah, Seth," Teddy said, directing his gaze at Noah, the middle son. "Barnabas changed his will a few months ago. He knew he was dying, and wanted to ensure you boys were all well looked after."

Fury bubbled up and burst out of Noah's mouth. "What, by leaving me penniless? By handing my land over to my brother who wouldn't know one end of a cow from the other?"

Jacob stared at him with sad eyes. It wasn't his doing, but that didn't stop Noah from being furious about the entire situation. *Did Jacob know the will had been changed?*

Noah's hands were white, from fisting them so tight. He had never been been so angry in his entire life. He had no idea what Barnabas had been thinking when he changed his will. And what was that about him knowing he was dying? That was news to Noah.

"Jacob, since you are already living in the main house, you may stay there. Noah, Seth,"

He'd heard enough. Noah shoved his chair back until it slammed against the floor, then stormed out of the lawyer's office, his temper a hot rage. What he would do now, he had no idea. But he couldn't help but wonder why his father had made such a stupid and heart wrenching decision. The thousand acres he'd been *gifted* on his twenty-first birthday, were supposed to be his for life. Now they'd been wrenched away from him.

He'd spent thc past nine years working hard on that land and was making a decent profit. Now he was being forced to hand it all over to his brother. Jacob knew absolutely nothing about running a ranch, and to Noah's mind, probably didn't want to either.

He'd never known his father to make such a foolhardy decision, and couldn't fathom what had caused it.

He left Teddy Black's office and headed to the saloon. He wasn't normally a drinking man, and the booze wouldn't help him think any clearer, but it might help calm his shattered nerves.

As he threw back his third whiskey, he saw Teddy enter the saloon.

"I've never heard anything so absurd in my entire life." Teddy had walked him to the nearest café and ordered strong black coffee. Noah had never been drunk before, but the reading of the will had totally shocked him.

Teddy waved to the waitress. "Another black coffee, please."

"This is so unlike Father," Noah said, his head starting to clear. "Why would he hand everything over to Jacob? It's so unfair."

The waitress refilled his mug then scurried away. "If you'd waited long enough, you would have heard the conditions." Teddy sounded annoyed. He'd been the family lawyer for as long as Noah could remember, and was more like an uncle to the three brothers. "Provisions have been made for your future. Seth's too."

Noah glanced up and stared at him. "What? Apart from wrenching *our* land out from under us?"

"No such thing will occur if you comply with the conditions I mentioned earlier. At least I tried to explain before you took off."

Dare he believe such a thing? What sort of conditions was Teddy talking about? Noah shook his head, which was finally clear. "What conditions are we talking about?" He stared suspiciously at at the older man. It wasn't bad enough he'd lost his father less than a week ago, now he had to deal with unknown conditions on a will that had been recently changed to benefit his older brother.

"Your father felt it was past time you settled down. To reclaim your land you simply have to marry in the next three weeks."

Noah nearly fell off his chair.

Angel's Pass, Montana

Mary Stanton stood at the rusty and worn out stove stirring the barely-there broth. This was the third batch of broth she'd made using the same bones, and was certain there would be little flavor this time around. There'd been one carrot and small piece of celery left in the pantry, but nothing more. She'd chopped them as finely as she could before adding them to the pot. She also tossed in some parsley from what was left of her herb garden, and a little salt and pepper for flavoring.

How she was meant to feed herself and her pa on such meagre pickings she had no idea, but it was expected of her. She scraped the mold off the five-day-old bread, and sliced it ready to toast. At least she had eggs to add to the moldy bread.

The kettle was on the stove, and Pa would get the last of the coffee. Until he was paid for this latest batch of pigs for slaughtering, that was the end of their supplies. Despite her constant requests for him to kill another one of the pigs for food, he refused. They were worth far more sold than for food, he'd said.

She would have to kill another chicken tomorrow or they would starve. They had few enough chickens as it was now. Less chickens also meant less eggs, but what was she supposed to do? She was slowly starving as it was.

Pa constantly raided her vegetable patch to feed the wretched pigs, which left her nothing to cook with. It was a vicious circle and a constant problem to keep food in their bellies. She sighed. Of course the pigs needed to be fed, but why did it have to be her lovely homegrown vegetables?

Scraping his boots at the bottom of the steps, Pa stepped into the washroom on the porch and washed himself. It was the one consolation he gave her. Mary couldn't stand the stench after he'd been working with pigs all day. He wasn't a bad man, her pa, but he was set in his ways, and rarely budged from his stance. It made her life extremely difficult.

She'd become so thin from the lack of food, she was often light-headed and had picked herself up off the floor on a number of occasions. As a hard working man, she put her pa ahead of herself when it came to meals.

By the time he entered the kitchen, she'd dished up the broth, giving herself a far smaller portion. The eggs were now ready, four for Pa, and one for herself, and she only needed to butter the toast with the scraping of butter they had left.

As hard as her life had become, this was her lot in life, and she'd never known anything different. Pa told her to get over it and accept what life dished out to her. She had no other choice.

Ma had died when she was ten, and Mary had run the household ever since.

"Mary," Pa said as he sat at the table and began to eat. "Remember Johnny Parsons – 'e used to come over with 'is Pa when you were a child."

She remembered him alright. Mary wasn't that small either – she was a teenager, and Johnny tried to kiss her on several occasions. He even tried to touch her where he had no right to be touching. The last time he came around, she'd made herself scarce, but he'd come looking for her and cornered her in the barn. He was evil through and through and she wanted no part of him.

She nodded, but would rather forget the horrible creature.

"Well, the boy's a man now, and 'e wants to marry you."

Her heart thudded. She hated to think what sort of man he'd grown into when he was so ghastly as a teenager.

"If I don't want to..." She let her words hang, but knew the conversation wouldn't end there.

Harry Stanton slammed his cutlery on the table and stared at his only child. "There ain't no choice," he bellowed. "Yer an old maid, I can't be supportin' yer forever." He picked up his fork and took another mouthful of food, then continued. "It's past time you was married. Johnny Parsons is visitin' Monday mornin' – make sure yer wearin' your Sunday best."

She looked down at the threadbare dress she was wearing. As much as she despised the man, perhaps he was her ticket out of the poverty she'd been living in for years. Mary straightened her shoulders. *Was she so desperate she would sink so low?* The man was despicable. He was a letch, and God only knew what she'd let herself in for if she married him.

She swallowed back the emotion that threatened to overtake her. “Yes, Father,” she said quietly, knowing there was no other choice.

Noah sat across the desk from Teddy, bogged down with worry. “How am I going to find a wife in such a short time?” He’d barely slept these past nights, and had no solution to his problem. “I can’t lose my ranch – I just can’t.”

Teddy shuffled some papers around on his desk. “There’s no way around it. Barnabas wanted you married, and when he found out his heart was failing, decided this was the only way.”

Noah stared at him with this new revelation. “Why didn’t he tell us he was dying?” He slammed his fist on the desk. “At the very least he could have warned us he’d changed his will. Jacob is even more upset than me and Seth.”

Reaching for a file, Teddy briefly read the papers inside. “I might have a solution to your problem,” he said, fingering the paper in front of him. “Have you ever heard of a proxy marriage?”

“No, never. What does it entail?”

“Well, to start, you don’t have to be together to get married.”

Noah raised his eyebrows. “That’s weird.”

Teddy wriggled in his seat. "You do still need to get together, but the marriage can be in two different places."

"So that means…"

"If we can find someone willing to marry you, even for only one year, you can keep your land." Teddy stared at him, no doubt waiting for an answer.

For a moment there, Noah thought his problem might be solved, but he didn't know any women. He'd been too busy working his land to socialize, especially out of town. And locally, any available women were snapped up in a hurry.

As if he could read Noah's mind, Teddy continued. "I have a sister who lives in Angel's Pass. It's not too far away, about two days on the train."

Noah stared at him. "You want me to marry your sister?" He was incredulous. Unless this sister was far younger than Teddy…

"No, Son. My sister is nearly double your age." He chuckled. "But she knows a young lady who fits the criteria of being your wife. She's living in dire circumstances and could use your help."

Noah listened carefully as Teddy explained further. The condition of having to only stay married to this proxy bride for a year sounded like a good idea. Noah wasn't interested in marrying, and never had been, but his hand had been forced.

Mary sat at the back of the church, along with Pastor Allenby, and listened carefully as Judith Hathaway explained the situation. The young man in question, Noah Adams, was a family friend to Mrs Hathaway's brother, she said.

While she hadn't seen him for many years, the older woman assured her Noah was an upstanding citizen, a hard worker, and a God-fearing man.

All the things Johnny Parsons was not.

Mary was assured of a safe and secure home, and after the twelve months, she would be well compensated for her trouble.

This was to be a marriage of convenience, and nothing more.

Besides helping herself, she would be helping a deserving young man reclaim what was already rightfully his. It would be forced from his hands without her help. "Take some time to think about it," Mrs Hathaway said in that reassuring voice that Mary found so calming. "I know it must be a difficult decision."

Mary's head shot up. Difficult? The choice between the lecherous Johnny Parsons, and the God-fearing man Mrs Hathaway had described? There really was no choice. She stared at the older woman, straightened her shoulders, and opened her mouth.

"No time needed. I'm in a difficult spot myself, so the timing is perfect," she said. "When do I leave?"

Mrs Hathaway stared at her – she knew Mary's situation, everyone in Angel's Pass knew. But still, she seemed rather shocked at Mary's immediate acceptance. Did she honestly think Mary would pass up such an opportunity? The chance to leave her wretched and soul destroying past behind?

"Well, I didn't expect that," Judith Hathaway said, clearly taken aback. She turned to the pastor. "When can you perform the ceremony?"

He scratched his head. "I guess we could do it now except we don't have a proxy to stand in for Miss Stanton."

Mrs Hathaway grinned. "My adult son is waiting outside for me. Would he do?" She was out of her seat before the pastor could answer, and in less than twenty minutes, Mary Stanton was no longer a single woman. It was going to get some getting used to being called Mrs Noah Adams.

Chapter Two

Mary stepped off the train wearing the only decent dress she owned. It was the same dress she'd been married in.

She carried a small carpetbag which held a few personal items such as her hairbrush and toiletries, Nothing else she owned was worth packing. Her only bonnet was on her head, but was doing a poor job of holding her hair in place after the long trip.

As people disembarked after their journey, Mary wondered if they felt as fatigued as she did. Sleeping upright was not an easy task, and it would be nice to lay her head down on a soft pillow in a comfortable bed.

Her new husband had wired money for her ticket and food. Mrs Hathaway had made all the arrangements for her. And while her father and Johnny Parsons were most unhappy, there wasn't a thing they could do about it – she was twenty-six after all.

Father was annoyed but understood, while on the other hand, Johnny was furious. She couldn't believe the rant he went into when he'd arrived the next morning to take her to town and marry her. If she didn't have the paperwork, she wasn't convinced either man would believe her.

As she glanced about, Mary breathed a sigh of relief. Now to find her husband, a man whom she'd never met, didn't even know existed until a few days ago, and had no idea what he looked like. How would she identify him? Her heart pounded and she felt light-headed. Not wanting to waste his money, she had skipped breakfast, not to mention supper last night – the prices in the dining cart were beyond atrocious, so she made do with a cup of tea. Mary stumbled as she headed toward the wooden bench at the other end of the platform.

Without warning, she felt a hand wrap around her arm. "Are you alright, Miss? Let me help you to the seat." A man supported her and guided her to the bench she'd spotted earlier. She glanced up at him, and had to almost tilt her head back to see him properly. He was solid, but not fat, and his blond hair was neatly trimmed.

Most of all, Mary noticed what an incredibly kind man he was. If her husband was even half as kind, she'd be very happy. "Thank you," she finally managed. "I haven't eaten since… oh dear, I guess it was lunchtime yesterday."

He looked her up and down. His expression one of shock. "Why not, if you don't mind me asking?" he said with a quiet voice.

Mary glanced down at her gown, and flicked away an invisible piece of cotton. Was it any of his business? Then again, perhaps he was just trying to help. "I, I was trying to save my new husband's money. It's alright," she added. "I'm used to not eating."

His shocked expression said it all. "Mary? Mary Stanton?"

She studied him. This was Noah Adams? "My name is Mary Adams," she said bluntly. "I guess you must be Noah."

They sat there quietly, assessing each other, but saying nothing for a few minutes. "I'll collect your luggage and then we'll go to the café and get you some food." He looked far from happy, but Mary couldn't fault his concern.

"This is everything I have," she said. "The rest wasn't worth bringing."

He nodded, but seemed confused. She wasn't surprised. What bride arrives to meet her new husband with only the clothes she's standing in? At least the gown she wore was presentable. It had been a gift provided by the church back at Angel's Pass, and one she was very grateful for. She hadn't been to church for years because Pa refused to take her. When she was old enough to manage the buggy alone, she was determined to go, Pa or no Pa. She'd been embarrassed at her state of dress, but remembered something her mother had told her years earlier. *The good Lord does not judge us by the clothes we wear, but by the love in our hearts,* and so she'd gone anyway.

The following week the pastor asked her to stay back after the service ended, and she'd been presented with the most beautiful gown she'd ever laid eyes on. The young woman it belonged to had outgrown it, he told her, and she could see it was still in perfect condition. To Mary it was more precious to her than a handful of gold.

When she glanced across, Noah was staring at her, and must surely think her mad. Or perhaps he wondered what he'd gotten himself into – a bride with no belongings. "I'm sorry," she said, then stood, waiting for him to guide her to their destination.

Instead he smiled. “Don’t be sorry,” he said. “At least this way we’re helping each other.” He hooked his arm through hers and they headed out of the train station and down the road to a small café.

Despite her refusals, he ordered a meal of roast lamb and vegetables for the both of them. Mary hadn’t realized how hungry she was until the food arrived. Drinks arrived soon after – coffee for Noah, tea for Mary. As she looked down into her plate, she couldn’t recall how long it had been since she’d eaten such a feast. She blinked back tears of joy. Was this what married life would be like for her? A proper meal every day?

“Is everything alright?” Noah Adams, a total stranger, seemed more concerned for her welfare than her own father had been for as long as she could remember. It made her heart ache.

She couldn’t tell him she’d been starved for as long as she could remember, not only for food but for affection. “I, I’m just a bit overwhelmed, is all,” she finally said, then picked up her cutlery.

“The food is good here,” he said. “I don’t come often, but when I do, the food is always great.” He cut a piece of the lamb and took a mouthful. “Delicious,” he said.

They ate their meal in silence until Noah had finished, and she pushed the remainder of hers away. She wasn’t used to eating such a vast amount of food, and simply couldn't manage it. He ordered them each a dessert of cherry cobbler. When she protested, he justified it by saying the meal was a celebration of their marriage. This was far more food than Mary would eat in an entire week back home, and despite eating little of it, felt like she might burst.

Noah studying her remaining food was not lost on Mary. But he said nothing.

Finally, he stood. "I'll take you to the mercantile to shop for clothes and whatever other supplies you need. While you're there, I'll go back for the wagon."

They strolled up the road, his arm hooked through hers, and Mary felt more relaxed than she had in a long time. Years.

Noah introduced her to Albert and Elizabeth Dalton who owned the mercantile. "I'm so happy Noah has finally married," Elizabeth told her. "It's about time. Now, you get some decent supplies for meals. That boy lives on baked beans and bacon, I swear."

She piled up the box with bread, potatoes, vegetables, cheese, flour, sugar, oats, milk, butter, and other staple items, then went looking for clothes. "These are our most popular day gowns," Elizabeth said pointing to a rack. "If you need undergarments, you'll find them over there," she said, pointing to a corner in the back of the store.

Choosing three of the cheapest gowns she could find, along with two nightgowns, Mary took them to the front counter. She also selected some undergarments. If he was only keeping her for a year, Mary didn't want to overtax Noah with expenses. Especially on their first day.

It wasn't long and he arrived back with the wagon. "I don't know what stores you have at home," she said. "Can you check what I've bought and tell me what else we need?"

"There are a few tins of baked beans," he said, and Elizabeth grinned. "You probably need to get a piece of bacon, but other than that, you've probably got everything else we'll need," he said, glancing in the box.

"Eggs?" she asked, not sure if he had chickens or not.

"There's more than enough with the dozen or so chickens we have. I've been selling eggs to Elizabeth, I've had so many."

After the purchases were added to his account, Noah began loading the items onto his wagon. "I don't come into town often, so make sure you've got everything you need," he told her. She assured him she did, but without having made any meals for him, Mary really had no idea.

It wasn't long before they were on their way to her new home.

They hadn't discussed his property, and as they passed under the archway to Broken Arrow Ranch, her surprise was obvious. She was brought up on a small farm, she told him, nothing of this proportion.

It took nearly twenty minutes from the archway to their ranch house, and her look of astonishment was priceless.

"I'm guessing your farm wasn't this big?"

She shook her head. "Nothing like it. Pa has about thirty acres, and most of that was for the pigs. Even our house was tiny. We barely had room for the two of us."

She glanced at him and he raised his eyebrows. "Are you serious?"

He was surprised when she nodded.

As they pulled into her new home, Noah glanced across at his bride. She sure was pretty, but was far too thin. If she starved herself like she'd done on the way to Halliwell, was it any wonder she was nothing but skin and bone. He hoped to soon remedy that.

He'd embarrassed her back at the train station, and for that he was truly sorry. Asking about the rest of her luggage was far from diplomatic, but he hadn't stopped to think. Teddy had told him Mary's situation wasn't good, but he hadn't really thought about what that meant. He should have asked so he knew what he would be dealing with.

Honestly though, was it even his business? That was in her past. What was important was their future. Determined to make her life easier, he lifted her down from the wagon and swooped her up into his arms. She was so light, he barely knew she was there. "Welcome to your new home," he said, staring into her face.

She wriggled about in his arms. "What are you doing? Put me down," she squealed. "Please?"

His new bride looked terrified. What had she been through in her past? "It's traditional," he said gently, trying to reassure her, then proceeded to open the door to their home and carried her across the threshold. Once inside he put her gently to the floor. She glanced about, a smile forming on her face.

"It's beautiful," she said. "I've never seen anything so lovely."

Really? His ranch house was quite basic. Three bedrooms, a kitchen, and sitting room, and a small bathroom. She wandered through the cabin, glancing about as she went. She almost ran into the kitchen and the look of amazement on her face was almost his undoing. Exactly where had she come from?

Okay, he knew she'd lived in Angel's Pass, the same place Teddy's sister lived. She rushed over to the stove, and squatted down, opened the oven doors to look inside, her eyes wide with amazement. Exactly what had she expected?

Then she bolted to the sink, and turned on the faucet. "Running water? You have running water?" Her eyes filled with tears. "No more carting buckets from the well."

His heart sank. This woman, this Mary Adams, whom he had married, had lived a dreadful life. He'd rescued her, just as she had rescued him.

"Let me show you the bathroom," he said. "There's running water there too." That was enough for tears to flow down her cheeks, and he rushed to her side. He wiped her tears away, then pulled her to him. The last thing he'd expected was to have his new bride distressed within minutes of arriving at her new home.

The home she would stay in for twelve months. When he wrapped his arms around her, she molded into him, and he felt like they'd known each other forever. His heart thudded. He wasn't sure how he would give her up after twelve short months. He already felt like they belonged together.

"I, I'm sorry," she said, pushing herself away from him and swiping at her tears. Even with her eyes red and puffy she was beautiful. Far too skinny, but beautiful nonetheless.

She suddenly turned and walked away, continuing her exploration of his cabin. Their cabin. Before she reached the bathroom, she stopped in the doorway to the main bedroom. He watched as she stared into the room, then swallowed. What was she thinking? Perhaps she didn't want to sleep with him? It pained him to think it, but he wouldn't force her. Even if she was his wife.

"Pretty quilt," she suddenly said, then scampered off toward the bathroom. "Ooooh," she squealed. "This is lovely." She ran over to the porcelain bath, and ran her hands over it. "I'm more used to a tin bath out on the porch. It gets pretty cold in the winter."

What sort of monster makes a young woman bathe outside in the winter? He opened his mouth to ask, but changed his mind. She would tell him if she wanted to, and there was no way he'd force the information out of her.

"Towels are in the cupboard," he said. "You'll find soap in there too. You can have a bath any time you want." He watched her expression change from distress to one of wonderment.

"Any time?" She ran over and hugged him. "I'm going to like it here," she said as she relaxed into him.

There was no doubt in his mind he was going to like having her here. And that was the last thing he should be thinking.

After taking all the supplies into the house, Noah left her to it. He had far to much to do, he'd said. He had lost several hours already, not that he'd blamed her. He made sure she knew how truly grateful he was to her for stepping up to marry him, sight unseen.

"Mrs Hathaway vouched for you," she told him. "That was enough for me. She's a lovely lady. Trustworthy too." Mary was more than grateful to the woman, and could never repay her for her generosity. Even if she was only promised a year in this wonderful cabin.

She made herself a promise right there and then, never to return to her father's property. She'd only been here a short time, and already felt rich. Mary swallowed. Did she really want to leave after a year? But that was the contract she'd signed. Stay married to Noah for one year, and receive a nice stipend for her trouble.

It was enough to set her up for life, to get her on track when he set her free.

She opened all the cupboard doors in the kitchen, deciding where to store what items. She had never seen so much food before in her life. Even when Mother was alive, they lived hand to mouth on a daily basis. Mary had never known any different. She packed everything away, then thought about what she would make for supper. With all this produce and other food items, she was in heaven. No more boiling bones for days on end to make a meal from nothing. Not that she intended to waste food – that would never do. But to know what she cooked would actually fill her husband's belly, and hers, was satisfaction itself.

The first thing she did after packing everything away, was put pots of water on to boil. Noah said she could take a bath any time she wanted, and by golly, she wanted one right now. Mary bit her lip. That felt so selfish when surely there was plenty to be done.

Instead she began cleaning the house. It wasn't filthy, but it wasn't as clean as it would have been if she'd been living here before. After washing all the floors, she wiped down all the counter tops, the table, and cleaned the bathroom. She also stripped the beds of their sheets and replaced them with fresh sheets. Tomorrow she would wash them all.

By the time she finished, it was time to make supper.

She began by making a batch of biscuits. It had been ages since she'd made them, simply because they'd run out of flour and Father refused to allow her to put anything on credit at the mercantile. Never had food been at her fingertips like it was now. But would that always be the case? Perhaps she shouldn't get comfortable with the situation, because you really never did know.

Glancing out the window, she noticed Noah riding in from across the paddock. That meant she didn't have long to prepare his supper. She carefully sliced the bacon and put it in the frying pan, then cracked eggs in the pan next to it. Mary had no idea how big an eater Noah was, although he put away that big meal at lunch. She cooked four eggs for him and one for herself.

It was pleasing to have fresh bread, and not have to worry about how old the bread was.

She cooked the toast on the fire, and by the time Noah had cleaned up, his meal was ready. She placed the biscuits in the center of the table, with a small plate of butter next to it. His coffee was already waiting for him, and she served his meal the moment he sat down.

"This looks amazing, Mary," he said. "I'm not used to this sort of supper."

She felt warm all over. “It’s not much,” she said. “Tomorrow I can make stew since I’ll have more time.” She shrugged as he reached for a biscuit.

“Please sit down, you’re making me nervous,” he said, taking a mouthful of the still-warm biscuits. “You’re an amazing cook, Mrs Adams,” he said with a grin. He pulled the biscuit away from his mouth and studied it. “These are different.”

“They’re cheese biscuits,” she said. “I’m going to enjoy cooking real food for you.” The moment the words were out of her mouth, she wanted to take them back.

“Real food?”

“You…” How much should she tell him? “You have lots of ingredients. I didn’t have those back home.”

He nodded thoughtfully, and took another mouthful of the biscuit. “Either way, they’re delicious. I am certain of one thing – I’m going to enjoy your cooking.”

This man was so kind. She already didn’t want to leave, let alone after twelve months. Mary vowed to put her despair aside. She had signed a contract to leave in one year, and that’s exactly what she needed to do. Whether she wanted to or not.

Chapter Three

Noah helped Mary dry their supper dishes. She was exhausted, he could see it all over her face. "Did you enjoy your bath?" he suddenly asked, remembering their earlier conversation.

She shook her head. *She didn't enjoy her bath?*

"I didn't have one. I decided to clean the house instead."

"But you were looking forward to a bath." Why did she clean instead of relaxing? Unless… please Lord no. It was looking more and more as though Mary had been treated more like a slave than a daughter. She hadn't said much except to say she looked after her father. What kind of father treats his child in such a way?

He dried the last of the dishes, then insisted she have a bath. Mary protested, but he rebuffed her and ensured she took one before bed.

"Let me carry the pots of water to the bathroom for you," he said, and that's exactly what he did. He dumped the hot water into the bath.

"It's like a mansion here. You even have proper floors," she said quietly when she was in the bathroom.

His heart thudded in his chest. What on earth had his wife endured? He pulled her to him and enveloped her. She seemed so scared and incredibly vulnerable. He ran his hand through the water that filled the bath, checking the temperature. It seemed about right, and he turned off the cold water faucet. "Grab a towel from that cupboard," he said. "There is soap on the bath, or you can get a fresh cake of soap from the same cupboard."

He turned and left her alone.

It seemed like forever before his new wife came out of the bathroom in one of her new nightgowns. She looked fresh and smelled wonderful, but she also looked weary. He'd sat reading his bible while she bathed, something he did every night.

"Did you enjoy your bath," he asked when she sat down opposite him. "You look more relaxed."

"It was wonderful," she said. "Especially being inside, away from the cold evening air."

She leaned back in the chair, and was soon sound asleep. Noah put aside his bible, then went to the bedroom and turned back the bedding. When he carried her to bed, she didn't so much as flinch.

He stood staring down at her for a very long time. He wondered what his wife had been through, and how long it was going to take for her to recover from the atrocities she'd endured.

Mary opened her eyes to the early morning light of dawn.

She glanced about trying to work out where she was – this place was not familiar. As she rolled over, she gasped at the sight of Noah in her bed. Well, really it was his bed, but she had no idea how she'd gotten there. The last thing she recalled was making herself comfortable in the sitting room after her luxurious bath.

As hard as she tried, she couldn't recall being moved. Could Noah have brought her to bed? It was the only explanation she could come up with. It was a moot point now anyway, so she needed to move forward.

She slid silently out of bed, trying not to wake her new husband. She snatched up her clothes and hurried to the bathroom where she dressed and prepared for the day. She pinned her hair up out of the way, and headed to the kitchen.

Mary sighed. It was a magnificent kitchen and she knew it would bring her great joy in the days and weeks to come. She was certain Noah had no idea how much happiness his home had already given her.

She shook herself. Now was not the time to stand around daydreaming. She had fires to light and a meal to cook before her husband awoke. If he was anything like her Pa, it wouldn't be long and he'd be up looking for something to eat.

She opened the door to the stove – there were still bright embers in there, but not enough to cook with. She threw in some twigs and prodded at it, to get it going, then filled the kettle with the faucets. How wonderful it was to have running water. It wasn't long before the fire was burning nicely.

Mary peeled some potatoes and cut them into small pieces, then threw them in the frying pan with an onion, then chopped some bacon into tiny pieces. She then a found a large bowl and filled it with flour, sugar, eggs and milk. Pancakes were this morning's breakfast. The potatoes would take far longer than the pancakes, so she decided not to cook those until Noah appeared. He seemed a reasonable man, unlike her Pa, and she was certain he'd be happy to drink his coffee while the pancakes cooked.

Was that true? She slumped down into a kitchen chair. She really had no idea what her husband was like. Yesterday he appeared to be kind-hearted, but was that all for show? She lay her head in her hands as she pondered the question. At least here there was food aplenty, and neither of them would starve.

She startled as he touched her shoulder. “Good morning,” he said gently, then leaned down to look at her. “Are you sick? Should I call the doctor?”

Her heart fluttered. It seemed she was correct – he was a kind man, and she needed to keep that in mind. “I’m fine,” she finally said. “Just thinking was all.” And she was. She was thinking about her new situation and her new husband, but couldn’t tell him that.

She suddenly stood and went to check on the potatoes. “Sit down and I’ll finish fixing your breakfast.”

He loitered about, looking rather awkward. “I don’t normally eat breakfast,” he told her.

She studied him. “Is that because you can’t be bothered making it?”

“Something like that.” He grinned at her and his face lit up. He was far more handsome than she’d originally believed, and now that he was more relaxed with her, she could see it. "Did you sleep well?"

She placed his coffee in front of him. "Sit down. And yes, I did, thank you. I guess you carried me to bed? You could have left me on the chair for the night."

His head shot up and he stared at her. "I would never treat you that way." He looked annoyed and took a mouthful of coffee while she made the pancakes. She stirred the potato mix then flipped the pancakes.

When she turned back around, he was staring at her. Was he trying to fathom her? There wasn't much to learn – what ever he needed or wanted, she would do. That's how it's always been for her.

She dished his breakfast onto his plate, then dished hers out. She added all the additional pancakes onto a separate plate and placed it in the center of the table. "There are left over biscuits from last night if you want some."

He glanced up at her. "You do know there's enough food here to feed a small village, right?" He grinned, then tucked into his meal again. "This is good," he told her as he wiped his mouth on the linen napkin. Suddenly he put down his cutlery. "Why aren't you eating?" His demeanor suddenly changed from happy to concerned.

Mary glanced down at her plate and shrugged her shoulders. She never ate until Pa finished in case he was still hungry. She wasn't sure she should tell Noah that. He might not understand.

"I'm not eating any more until you begin." He sat ramrod straight and stared at her until she felt uncomfortable. "You're already far too skinny. You need fattening up." He frowned and continued to stare.

Under his scrutiny, she began to eat, so he resumed as well. "I'll be working in the front paddock today," he said. "I should be back for lunch around noon. Can you manage that?" He took another mouthful of food. "Has anyone ever told you what a wonderful cook you are?"

No, they never had. It wasn't like Pa to compliment anything she did. "Not really," she said, not wanting to admit too much. "What do you want for your noon meal?" She thought for a moment, trying to remember what she had available to cook. "I could make some vegetable soup?"

"Can't wait," he said as he finished up his food. Taking a last mouthful of coffee he stood. "I really must go. I've normally left by now." Noah walked toward her and Mary stood. Standing in front of her, he stared down into her face.

"Has anyone ever told you how beautiful you are," he asked quietly. His hands came up and cupped her face with his hands. He stared down into her face for the longest time. He was going to kiss her, she was certain of it, and her heart thudded. Mary wasn't sure how she felt about that, after all, they'd known each other for less than a day.

On the other hand they were married, and he had every right...except they'd both agreed to a marriage of convenience.

As if he suddenly came to his senses, Noah's hands dropped away and he stepped back. "I'll be off then," he said abruptly, then headed toward the front door.

She quivered at the sudden loss of his hands on her, which was stupid, she knew it was. Until now, no one had paid any attention to her. Except Johnny Parsons, and that was for a totally different reason. He'd tried to force her, to sully her, and would have walked away afterwards. If Pa hadn't come looking for her, called her name when he did, goodness knows what might have happened. She shivered at the thought.

Mary had a little over a few hours until Noah would be back, and there was time enough to prepare the soup. She would also make sandwiches with the cheese she'd bought at the mercantile.

Once the soup was on the stove and cooking, she'd start on supper. Beef stew with dumplings. Already she felt like a queen. The food she'd made in the short time she'd been here would have to last a week or more at Pa's. She wondered how he was faring without her, then shook herself. He was ready to barter her off to Johnny Parsons – for what she didn't know – so she needed to get him out of her head.

With the meals prepared, she went to check out the wash room. It was a nice day with a decent breeze, and the sheets she'd removed from the beds yesterday needed washing. As she stood staring, tears rolled down her face. After spending more than ten years washing in the tin bath tub, wringing everything by hand, she was overwhelmed with the wooden barrel that sat on the large shelf. There was a washboard, and also a device on the side, to wring the water out of the washing.

She'd heard of such things, but never had Mary seen such an amazing device herself. Even in this tiny washroom, there was running water. How could she ever leave this place with all of its wonder? She really didn't know if she ever could. Mary reminded herself once more that she'd willingly signed the contract.

Her heart was already breaking. How would she feel when she had to walk away from all this, and especially Noah? She didn't dare to even imagine.

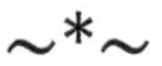

In all the years since Ma had died, Mary hadn't once felt lonely. Of course she'd grieved for the loss of her dear mother, but that was a totally different thing. Grief and loneliness were two totally different things.

Pa had never really cared for her, and if she didn't know better, she'd wonder if she was even his daughter. His only interest in her was to have food on the table and the house clean. His pigs were far more important to him, and it broke her heart. She'd decided years ago to distance herself from him, because it was detrimental to her wellbeing to do otherwise.

In the few hours since Noah had left to go to the front paddock, she'd felt hollow. Already she was missing him, which was totally ridiculous. She didn't know the man, and he didn't know her. If she could keep it that way, it would be far easier for the both of them to walk away this time next year.

The back door slammed and she knew he was back. Mary gave the soup a last stir and pulled two bowls out of the cupboard. His sandwiches were made, and the kettle boiled, ready to make his coffee. Noah went straight to the bathroom to wash up, then appeared in the kitchen. He was a sight to behold. "I'm back," he said quietly, then walked over to her and stood staring at her.

It unnerved her, and she wondered what he was thinking. "Sit down," she said suddenly, before he had a chance to say or do anything else. "Your soup is ready." She dished out a large bowl of the hearty vegetable soup, and placed it in front of him. He reached for a sandwich.

"It looks good," he said, taking a mouthful of food. "It's nice not having to worry about meals." He tucked into the soup and didn't speak again until his bowl was empty. "You're not eating," he said bluntly.

"There's more," she said, then stood and refilled his bowl without waiting to find out if he was still hungry. He was a man – of course he'd want more. She placed the bowl in front of him and walked away. He grabbed her wrist before she could get far. Mary turned to face him.

"You need to eat," he said, staring up at her.

She contemplated him. Was he concerned for her health, or was he worried what other people would think when they saw his *skinny wife*, as he'd called her yesterday? "I've survived so far," she said, then pulled out of his grip. "More coffee?" As she walked away, she heard him sigh.

"I'm fine," he said, then tucked into his second bowl of soup.

Mary sat at the other end of the table and began to eat. Noah watched her every move. She wasn't sure she could spend the next twelve months being scrutinized. No one else ever cared what she did – why should he?

When they'd finished their meal, she cleared the dishes away and placed them in the sink. She had running water. Mary thought she may never get over that. She'd spent far too many years carting buckets of water from the well to the house. She still had to boil the water to wash the dishes, to have a bath, and to do the laundry, but she didn't care.

Despite him describing it as a ranch house, Noah's house was a mansion in her eyes. She felt far richer than she ever imagined possible. She startled when he came up behind her.

"I'll be off then," he said, and his closeness warmed her. What would it be like to have him hold her like he wanted her? She shivered. She needed to keep such foolishness out of her head. A marriage of convenience was just that. Mary was there to cook and wash for him, and to keep up appearances. He was forced into marriage to keep his property, there was nothing more to it.

Except for Mary, it felt like there was. It was a silly notion, and she knew it. Perhaps if she pretended she was his housekeeper? She was promised a stipend when the contract was completed, and that would keep her going. She spun around to look at him, and brushed back a loose tendril that tumbled across her face.

He stared at her and his hand lifted but suddenly stopped. "I'll be back in time for supper," he said, then spun on his heels and left without another word.

Emptiness overwhelmed her.

Chapter Four

Mary had been here for nearly a month now. She'd kept her distance as much as possible, including sleeping in the spare room.

Not that her husband was happy about the fact, but if she couldn't have the man, she didn't want to be in his bed. Wasn't that for the best anyway? There were days when she was certain he'd regretted demanding a marriage of convenience. It was evident in the way he studied her sometimes, and the way he stood close by, but seemed to stop himself going further. Did he yearn for more?

Many times now she thought he was going to kiss her, or put his arms around her, but somehow he'd managed to stop himself. Deep in her heart she wished he wouldn't, but letting him would only make it harder when she had to leave. Instead she kept herself busy around the house.

She'd settled into a routine, and so had Noah. He'd mentioned the fact she was looking healthier than when she'd arrived. That was a good thing she supposed. Since arriving, she no longer felt lightheaded, and hadn't stumbled even once. She had Noah to thank for that.

She heard the back door slam, and could picture him taking off his sweaty hat and placing it on the rack at the door. He'd go straight to the bathroom and clean up before coming to her. It had taken forever to get Pa to do the same thing, and he'd done it reluctantly. Noah seemed to do it out of respect for her.

He came to her and kissed her on the forehead, something he'd recently begun to do. It sent a shiver through her every time. "I'm back," he said out of habit. She smiled. Mary had come to love those moments when he touched her, brief as they were. Of course there was nothing to them – it was simply Noah being friendly. She was after all, his wife.

"Anyone home," a strange voice called from the front door.

Noah sighed, then stepped away from her. "In the kitchen."

The moment she set eyes on the stranger she could see the familiarity. The two men had to be related.

"Mary," he said, turning to her, "This is my younger brother, Seth." Noah didn't seem terribly happy to see his brother. Was he ashamed of her?

Seth looked her up and down. "Steady on," Noah told him. "That's my wife you're ogling." He grinned then, and the mood seemed to be lightened.

The younger man laughed then stepped toward Mary and hugged her. "Welcome to the family." He sounded genuine, and it made her feel sad. She should have been happy at his words, and ordinarily she would. But when her marriage was nothing more than a pretense, how could she feel welcomed?

Suddenly he slapped Noah on the back. "You didn't tell me your wife was so beautiful. Is that why you've been hiding her away?" He grinned at her. The brothers were so similar to look at, and their grin almost identical. It was uncanny.

She felt heat creep up her neck and through her face. "Now look what you've done," Noah said jokingly. "You've embarrassed her." He came closer and put his arm around her shoulder and pulled her close.

Mary molded into him. It had been so long since Noah had held her this way, and she'd missed it. In spite of that, she had to keep in mind it was all for show. Did he want Seth to think they had a real marriage? That was the most likely scenario.

"Did you only come here to ogle my wife, or was there something you wanted?" Noah spoke in jest, she knew, but warmth flooded her at the thought of him being so protective of her.

"Have you eaten," she asked Seth. "I'm making pancakes."

He glanced at Noah and raised his eyebrows in question. "Pancakes? You didn't tell me you were being spoiled, big brother. How can I say no to such an invitation?"

Mary poured coffee for the two men who sat at the table talking about work, then began to prepare the pancakes. She felt eyes on her and glanced up to see Noah studying her. Had his brother's words triggered something in him? After all this time, did he have feelings for her, or was it jealousy?

His actions certainly hadn't shown any affection for her, not really, so it must be jealousy on Noah's part. Simply because Seth had shown some small interest in her. Funny, she hadn't seen him as the jealous type. But it was what it was.

Once the pancakes were ready, she placed them in the center of the table. They didn't last long, and if she didn't know better, she'd think Seth was starving. More likely he was starved for homecooked food, like Noah had been.

"Delicious," Seth told Mary. "You're a remarkable cook."

Noah stared at him. "Yes, she is, and you can't have her." He chuckled.

"So tell me," Seth asked after they'd finished eating. "How are you two getting on?" It seemed a strange question to ask and it had Noah and Mary staring at each other. Seth shrugged. "Oh, I know – you're newlyweds but it's not like you wanted to get married."

Noah stiffened, and Mary felt dismayed by his words. As though wanting to prove otherwise, Noah leaned over kissed her on the lips. The tingle she felt rumbled through her, and Mary wished he meant it instead of trying to prove something to his brother. He grinned, then winked at her.

If only he really meant it.

Seth shrugged. Had he seen through Noah's pretense? "I'm going to be in the same situation soon." Noah glared at him. "You know – because of Father's ridiculous condition in the will."

Mary suddenly stood and cleared away the dishes, leaving the men to retire to the sitting room. Only they didn't. Noah came up behind her and wrapped his arms around her. "He didn't mean anything by it," he whispered, and she nodded. She knew that, but Seth's words still stung.

Had he guessed at their situation? Or had Noah told him? Either way, it pained her to feel this way. She'd become so settled in her life here at Broken Arrow Ranch and didn't want to leave. If she was honest with herself, she had feelings for Noah. It was him she didn't want to leave. She would be happy wherever she lived, provided Noah was in her life.

Could she ever have a real marriage with Noah? It was highly unlikely.

"It's calving time." Noah took a sip of his coffee, and shoveled in some food. "My men will do the bulk, but I'll be working long hours for the next week or so." He glanced up at her. Mary was staring at him. "Dang cows wander off all over the place so we have to round them up. Not to mention getting in trouble. Sometimes we have to deliver them ourselves or risk losing them." Last season they lost six. Not a lot in the scheme of things on a property of this size, but every calf formed part of his livelihood.

He was determined not to let that happen again this year. He'd even put on more workers this time around.

Mary studied him over her mug. “I didn’t know you had anyone working for you.” She was frowning. With a property this size, of course he’d have workers “Do they live on the property?”

“Yes, of course. Did you honestly think I could manage a place this big without help?” Was she really that naive? “How big was your Pa’s property? Did he have help?”

She laughed, but not in a funny way. “Pa pay for workers? You are joking, right? We barely had money for food.”

Everything was beginning to make sense. She’d looked more than half starved and destitute when she’d arrived, and suggested she wore the only decent piece of clothing she’d owned. Of course she didn’t say it in so many words. “There’s a worker’s hut a couple of paddocks over. I like to keep my private life private. I certainly don’t want them ogling my beautiful wife.” He winked at her then reached out and touched her hand from across the table.

A shiver went through him. How many times now had he admonished himself for his stupidity in agreeing to a loveless marriage? A marriage of convenience? Just standing near to Mary was enough to set his hormones on edge. If she hadn’t taken to sleeping in the spare room from that second night, he would have ravaged her by now.

She was beautiful, sweet, naïve, and she was his wife. He abruptly pulled his hand away. What sort of fool was he? Every time he touched her only made him want her more. To torture himself was beyond foolish. Besides, Mary had no feelings for him. He was merely a meal ticket and a means to provide somewhere safe to stay. The minute their twelve month contract was up, he had no doubt she would put her hand out for the compensation, and would be on her way.

The thought of never seeing her again ripped at his heart.

"…for them?" His head shot up. What was she saying? He really didn't want to confess he'd been lost in his own thoughts, thinking about things he didn't want to admit.

"I, sorry. I missed half of that. Too busy day dreaming."

She stared at him. It wasn't like him, and she knew it. They might not be intimate, but she knew him intimately in most other ways. The times he came and went, what he wore, what he ate, and so much more.

They had a very good marriage, except for the fact… He glanced up. Why did his thoughts keep going back there? Perhaps because every blessed night he knew she was sleeping in the other room half undressed, and he couldn't touch her?

No, that wasn't it, and he knew it. He was… he shook his head trying to shake the thought away but it wouldn't leave him. He was more than a little fond of Mary. He was – he swallowed. He was falling in love with her.

"Should I make food for them?" She sighed, probably at his lack of concentration. Or had she seen through him? Read his thoughts? She'd probably run like the devil if she had. Mary was not interested in a real marriage with him. Truth be told, she never would be.

She'd told him bits and pieces of her former life. Well, not so much told as he'd read between the lines. He knew she had to cart water from a well into the house. He also knew she bathed outside in the cold, with absolutely no privacy. Her clothes were so dreadful she refused to bring even one item to her new home. Not to mention her state of health. It made him nauseous thinking about how pale and thin Mary was when she'd arrived. He'd rejoiced in watching her put on weight and grow stronger every day.

It had never been said, but it was clear to Noah she had been destitute. Left where she was, she might even have died. He couldn't bear the thought of never having met her.

No wonder she was happy now. If she left him, which she undoubtedly would, at least he could be thankful he'd given her a safe home and a better life.

He swallowed. Hard. His heart was aching beyond comprehension.

"Food for the men? You can if you want to, but it's not required. They have a bunk house where they can cook for themselves." He needed to concentrate on the conversation.

He waved a hand in the air. "Tomorrow perhaps. If you want to that is." Noah stood, keeping his eyes trained on his sweet wife. "I'm running late. I need to go."

Mary also stood and began to clear the dishes. "I won't be home for lunch today, or any other day this week." He stepped toward her and she straightened. Hesitating, Noah finally held her by the shoulders, and leaned in. She glanced up into his sapphire blue eyes, then stared at his lips. She licked hers.

Was she willing to kiss him? On the lips? The last time he did that, it was only for a moment, and only for Seth's benefit. It had taken him by surprise, and his entire body had filled with warmth.

He stared into her face, and his heart pounded. A zing went through him.

Mary gazed at him with anticipation.

He wanted this so badly his heart hurt. Instead he dropped his hands and kissed her forehead. Just like he'd done every other morning.

Noah turned his back on her and strode toward the door before he could change his mind.

Chapter Five

The moment Noah walked out the door, Mary let go of the breath she'd been holding and gazed after him. Tears rolled down her cheeks and she swiped them away.

Did he hate her so much that he couldn't so much as bring himself to kiss her? At least it proved she'd been right about his previous kiss – it had been totally for his brother's benefit.

Back home, Pa had never shown her any affection. Not any. At least there she knew where she stood. With Noah he was hot and cold. One moment he'd touch her hand, then abruptly pull it away, he'd start to kiss her then stop. She couldn't fathom whether he had feelings for her and was trying to deny them, or whether he absolutely no feelings for her, and was trying to force them on himself.

Either way, her heart was breaking. It had been her choice to retreat to the spare bedroom, but not once did Noah ask her to move back. He shown no sign of wishing she would. Had he asked, she'd have gone in a heartbeat, but after years of living it, Mary knew when she wasn't wanted.

Instead of dwelling on what could have been, or might have been, she decided to instead focus on the present. She pulled herself together and cleaned away the breakfast dishes, wiped down the table, then checked the pantry for supplies. It wouldn't be long and they'd have to go into town for more.

Recalling Noah's words about the calving, did that mean she would have to go alone? Urgh. She hated driving a wagon, or even a buggy. She'd had a little practice, but supplies were getting low, and soon enough, there would be no choice.

Instead of dwelling on the future, she concentrated on organizing supper. She'd killed a chicken yesterday, so could make a nice chicken roast for tonight. That way, there would be leftovers for his lunch tomorrow. She glanced outside. The sun was shining, and it looked inviting. She would take in some fresh air before beginning her day of cooking and cleaning.

Wiping away the last of her errant tears, Mary stepped outside. The warmth hit her, just as it did when Noah touched her, even for the briefest of moments. Shaking the thought away, she walked down the few steps and into the garden. At some point there had been a vegetable patch here. It wasn't tiny either, and could accommodate all their produce requirements if it were allowed to grow again. She wondered why Noah had let it go so badly.

She stared at the barren ground. Without thinking she dropped to the ground and began to run her fingers through what she was certain would once have been rows of vegetables. There was nothing there now, not even any so much as a dead root. She made up her mind there and then to buy some plants at the mercantile. Seeds would be cheaper, but plants would grow to full size far quicker.

Mary made a mental note to buy a nice assortment when she was there next. Excitement shivered through her. After the last time Pa had ripped out her carrots for the pigs, she hadn't bothered again. It was futile. She planted them in, he pulled them out.

She would get carrots, potatoes, beans, and perhaps parsnips. Maybe even corn. She was certain Noah wouldn't mind.

The wind picked up and a shiver went through her. Mary headed back inside, her mind full of possibilities.

Noah went straight to the washroom when he arrived home. The stench wasn't as bad as the pigs, but it wasn't good either. He stripped off his clothes, then walked through the house in nothing but his drawers.

Was he going to do this every day after calving? It was unsettling, and it took all her effort for Mary to look away.

He stood in the middle of the kitchen and breathed in their supper. "Smells good," he said, then went on his merry way as though nothing was amiss.

But it was amiss. Her husband stood near naked in the middle of the kitchen – his torso bare, and his muscles rippling. He was a fine specimen of man, and she could not touch him. Couldn't even hug him. She thought back to those first days when she arrived. He'd held her in his arms, and she'd felt safe, protected, but especially wanted.

She no longer felt wanted – except for her housekeeping skills. It broke her heart into tiny pieces.

Mary heard water running in the bathroom and busied herself with setting the table. If she knew what time Noah would be home each evening, she could have a bath ready for him.

At least he bothered with a bath. Pa rarely did, which made his stench even harder to bear.

"Oh Lordy," she said under her breath, and ran into the washroom. There sitting on the bench was a pile of freshly folded towels. There wasn't a single towel left in the bathroom for her husband to use.

She tapped on the door. "I'm sorry, Noah," she called as her heart raced. "I have the towels out here."

She was sure she could hear him laughing. "Come in."

Her hand wrapped tightly around the handle, Mary gingerly opened the door. There in the bathtub sat her husband, his chest lathered in soap. She quickly covered her eyes with her hand.

He chuckled. "How are you going to get to the cupboard like that," he asked, his mirth plain to hear. "Bring one over here will you?"

Her hand dropped from her face and she glared at him. "That wouldn't be proper," she said, then turned, ready to flee.

"Mary," he said gently. "I'm your husband. Of course it's *proper*." She glanced up to see a grin on his face, but it soon disappeared when she glared at him. What he was thinking, she would never know.

"It's not a proper marriage," she said firmly. "Which means it's not in line with propriety." Before he could say another word, she threw the towel across the room, then turned to leave.

"Good grief, Mary!" She'd never heard Noah angry before and spun around at the unfamiliar sound. "This is becoming ridiculous," he said softly, reverting back to his normal demeanor.

At the sight of the wet towel floating in the bath water, Mary suddenly stopped. *Had the towel connected with her husband? Had it harmed him?* His expression was one of annoyance, but he didn't seem to be injured.

"Please pass me a dry towel and *bring it* over here." He sounded more exasperated than anything, but Mary felt wary. Pa would have clipped her up the side of the head, but she didn't think Noah would do that to her. Would he? She braced herself and took a tentative step forward. "Now please, Mary." He reached under the water and removed the plug. Mary stood mesmerized watching the water swirl down the drain. Anything to stop looking at her husband in all his glory.

He cleared his voice and she suddenly leapt forward, handing over the towel and turning once again to leave. Her caught her by the wrist. “I think it’s time we talked, don’t you?”

“What about?” Her voice was small, and barely audible. Noah stared at her, then stood in all his nakedness, and it made her uncomfortable. She wanted to leave but he still had hold of her wrist. “I need to see to our supper.”

“It can burn for all I care,” he said quietly. “We need to talk about… our situation.” He finally took the towel and wrapped it around his waist, releasing her in the process.

Her heart pounded. Noah was letting her go. Sending her away.

She wasn’t ready to leave yet, if she ever would be, and she didn’t have the funds to set herself up somewhere else. Surely he didn’t intend to pay the stipend she was due at the end of their year together? They’d only been married less than six months.

Her mind was suddenly in overdrive. She had no skills – how could she get a job? Oh. Unless she found somewhere that needed a cook. Or a housemaid. She had plenty of experience with both.

Halliwell was a small town, but they had a saloon. Perhaps she could get a job there? She shook her head – that wasn’t what she wanted, she wanted to be here with Noah. Her pretend husband.

She shoved her fist in her mouth to stop herself from calling out, then fled from the room, leaving Noah to call after her.

Mary finished making the gravy with the juices from the chicken, and placed it in the jug on the table. "It smells delicious," Noah said as he leaned over to carve the roasted chicken. Mary dished out the roasted vegetables while he did so, and placed them on a plate in the center of the table.

The freshly baked bread was accompanied by a small tub of butter.

"You certainly know your way around the kitchen," he said lightly. It was as though their encounter in the bathroom never occurred. Mary passed him two dinner plates, and he began to dish up. "You know we need to talk," he said, handing her a plate of food.

Mary nodded but he was certain she hoped he would forget when it came time. He reached across the table and grasped her hand, then bowed his head. "Lord, we thank you for this food and for each other. Amen."

Mary stared at him long after he'd finished speaking. "It's cooked to perfection," he said, squirming under her scrutiny, then took another mouthful. "I've never eaten such a delicious meal," he said, then wanted to take it back. His wife had made so many wonderful meals since she'd arrived, and his comment might upset her.

She suddenly stood. "I have a pie in the oven," she said, snatching up the kitchen cloth. She lifted it out, placing it on the wooden board, then returned to the table.

"It feels like you're avoiding the conversation." He was certain she was.

"I have to go into town in the next day or so," she said, ignoring his words and completely changing the subject. "We're low on supplies."

"I haven't got time at the moment. We're still calving." She knew that, so why even suggest it?

She lifted her napkin and wiped at her soft lips. "I can go alone. I don't like driving a wagon though."

"Take the buggy. I'll hook up the horse before I leave in the morning."

She stared at him momentarily. "I can do it. I've done it before."

He opened his mouth to remind her once more of their impending conversation, but decided against it. Meal times should be relaxing not stressful, and he didn't want to spoil their dinner. Mary had worked hard to make this meal. He had no right to ruin it.

"I thought I'd plant a vegetable garden," she said out of the blue. "It looks like you've had one before."

He took the last mouthful of his food before answering. "I did, years ago. It wasn't worth the effort when I lived alone. I had far too much, and even giving my brothers a share, there was a glut. I finally let the plants die off."

Noah could see the annoyance on her face. Why did she care so much about a vegetable patch that had perished so long ago? It didn't make sense, but it was plain to see – his neglect of that piece of dirt upset her.

He reached across the table and covered her hand. "Why does that bother you so much?" He kept his voice quiet, gentle. His loud voice had upset her earlier.

Her eyes wide with astonishment at his question, she licked her lips before answering. His eyes followed her every move. "I had a magnificent vegetable patch back home. Pa ripped it out for the pigs." The last sentence was near-snarled. "We almost starved for those wretched creatures, and for what? Pa barely made a living out of them."

She suddenly snatched her hand away, then jumped up from the table. Mary turned her back to him and stood rigid for long moments. He was about to go to her when she turned to face him, and Mary's entire demeanor suddenly changed to one of defeat. "Those pigs were far more important than I ever was." She took a long shuddering breath and her eyes portrayed her sadness. "You saved me from that life."

She turned away again, this time her body shook, but it was the silence that was his undoing. He moved quietly toward her, not wanting to startle his wife, and slid his arms around her. "Mary," he said gently. "You're important to me. Very important."

She spun around in his arms, and he cradled her against his chest, her tears hot against his shirt. He leaned in and kissed her forehead, and she shivered. Noah's heart was breaking in two. What she had endured was unthinkable and he was determined she wouldn't go through any of that again.

It felt good with her so close to him, as though it was meant to be. They were meant to be. But there was still distance between them. They both knew it. He studied her as she snuggled into him and he ran his fingers through her hair, pulling it loose as he did so.

She glanced up at him, wiping at her errant tears. "I'm sorry," she suddenly said, then pulled away. "The pie is ready. Sit down." It wasn't a request, it was a demand. He watched as she composed herself, then continued as though nothing had happened. As though he hadn't held her just moments ago, as if his world hadn't titled.

He knew nothing would be the same for him again.

Chapter Six

Noah stood in front of his wife and cupped her face. He stared down into her eyes and his gaze lingered. How he longed to stay home, to sit down with her and talk. Finally he might get to know her. Then, and only then would they have a real marriage.

But it wasn't to be. Several cows were still calving, and had disappeared into the abyss. Noah and his men would spend the day trying to find those wayward cows and bringing them to safety.

"I really must go," he said with regret.

Regret for the words that hadn't passed between them last night, and for the sort of life Mary had lived before coming to Broken Arrow Ranch. She had hurried to bed soon after supper last night, and he was certain she felt embarrassed.

There was no need. The sins of the father were not the failings of the daughter. Mary was a victim, and certainly not responsible for anything that had occurred while under her father's roof. He felt himself stiffen at the injustice of it all. Dear, sweet Mary – she had not asked for that treatment, and had not deserved it. To live in poverty for most of her life was an abomination. Surely *someone* must have known her situation?

He mentally shook himself. What were they to do? Especially when she was a child? Short of remove Mary from her father's so-called care, there was little anyone could do. Had they done so, she would have ended up in one of those appalling orphanages. Then he would never have met her.

"Is everything alright," she asked in her quiet voice.

Noah pulled himself out of his thoughts. "Yes, of course," he said knowing it was a lie, then leaned in and kissed her gently on the cheek. He suddenly pulled her to him. He hadn't planned to do so, but he liked how it felt. Last night had made him feel all sorts of things he'd never felt before.

He stared into Mary's face. How he longed to kiss her lips. If holding her could elicit such delightful feelings, what would kissing her do? He dared not wonder.

Instead, he kissed her cheek again, then wrapped his arms tightly around her. "I'm really glad you came here, Mary," he whispered in her ear, then pushed her away. "I really must leave now." His horse waited out front, already saddled and ready to go.

It would be a long day, by all accounts, unless the missing livestock miraculously turned up safe and sound with little intervention. From many years of experience, Noah knew that would never happen. He reluctantly let her go, and strode to the door. With his hand on the handle, her turned back to face his wife, but she was already busy clearing away the breakfast dishes.

Carrying his saddlebags, he strolled out to Cinnamon, the Chestnut horse he'd had for more years than he cared to remember. Noah's horses came before himself, and even if he had no money for food, his horses never went hungry. He tried to shake away the distant memories, and mounted his horse.

He clicked his tongue and they were soon on their way.

The closer they got to the dam, the louder the sound. They had one very unhappy mama in distress somewhere nearby. "She's stuck in the mud at the edge of the dam," Joe told Noah. The old cowboy had been on Broken Arrow Ranch for more years than he cared to remember. At least that's what he always told Noah. He'd worked for Barnabas, Noah's father, back when the ranch had first been established, along with Clancy and Billy. Although to listen to Joe, Billy was a newcomer – he'd only been here for about twenty years.

The distraught lowing continued and it broke Noah's heart. He could see the calf's head pushing out, but with mama stuck, they could lose them both as they lay in several inches of water and mud. "We have to get her out," Noah said. "We're going to lose that calf, not to mention the cow." He snatched a roll of rope from his saddle and fashioned it into a lasso. "Okay fellas, get into position. We're going to save this calf."

Before another word could be said, Noah had lassoed the cow's front legs. Billy had her around the neck, Clancy had her back legs and Joe was on standby in case he was needed. It took all their effort, and quite a bit of time, but with everyone doing their bit, they soon had the stubborn cow unstuck.

It wasn't long before the precious calf was born. "Well if that weren't an effort and a half," Clancy said. They waited around to make sure the calf was fine, and moved them further away from the dam. Noah felt like he'd already done a day's work. They'd only been out and about for a couple of hours.

By the time he arrived home in the semi darkness, Noah was covered in mud. He stripped off in the washroom as he always did, and made his way to the bathroom.

He strode through the kitchen.

It was quiet and Mary wasn't about. Nothing was on the stove cooking. That was very unlike Mary. Then again, he'd been spoiled by her cooking efforts, and they were likely having bacon and eggs or some such easy meal tonight. Not that they'd done that since she first arrived.

Strange.

He then realized the chickens were running around outside and not contained in their pen. Mary always had them locked up by now.

Noah continued to the bathroom, but something wasn't right. There was always food cooking when he arrived home, the stove was hot, and the ranch house was warm and welcoming.

Tonight there was none of that.

Where was Mary?

He quickly washed himself down and dressed in clean clothes. Somewhere in the back of his mind was the memory Mary had told Noah she was doing something special today. He was so obsessed with the calving, he couldn't recall what it was.

He checked the spare room in case she was lying down having a rest. Before he even checked, he knew she wouldn't be there. Mary never shirked her responsibilities. Where was she?

Now he was getting concerned. Had she left him? He stood in the middle of the room in disbelief. Mary wouldn't do that to him, not without talking to him first. Besides, where would she go? By her own admission, she was destitute. She had no money, and didn't know the area. Not really.

He was beginning to panic and had to force himself to slow his breathing. He knew in the back of his mind there was something he was forgetting. Something Mary had told him. He sat on the side of the bed and forced himself to think. What had she said last night? What was the conversation they'd had? Something about supplies?

His breath caught in his throat – she was taking the buggy to town. Alone.

Noah scrambled to his feet, then ran out to the barn. The buggy was gone. What had happened to his beautiful wife? He dared not begin to imagine.

"I'm sorry, Cinnamon," he told the horse as he saddled her so soon after his recent ride. "We have to find Mary."

He collected Seth along the way as well as his other brother Jacob, and they took the main road into town. It was the only route Mary knew to travel.

"We'll find her," Seth said, sounding not very convincing, then leaned across from his horse and patted Noah's back. "I know how much she means to you."

Seth was right, Mary meant more than life itself, but Noah had never told her so. Was it too late to tell her?

She could be dead, and he'd never get his chance. He choked back his emotions.

"Over there," Jacob shouted, and pointed to a ditch. The buggy was tipped on its side, the agitated horse still attached, but there was no sign of Mary. She hadn't even made it into town – there were no supplies in sight.

Noah gasped. That meant she'd been out here alone most of the day. While he searched about, his brothers righted the buggy and checked over the horse. It was spooked but mostly uninjured.

Jacob held onto the reins to stop her running away.

"Mary!" Even with the flame brightly lit, the light from the lantern was still quite dull out here in the bushes. "Mary!" Noah called again.

"Mary," Seth shouted, then shushed his brother. "Mary?"

"Noah?" Her small voice broke through the silence.

The two men ran toward the sound and stared down to where she lay. "Mary," Noah said, his voice cracking. "I, I thought you were dead," he said.

"I might have broken my ankle," she said quietly. "But I'm alive." Noah handed his lantern to Seth then scooped up his wife and gently carried her out of the bushes, his heart thudding. He could easily have lost her today. His biggest regret was never having told Mary he loved her.

"I'm fine," Mary told him firmly. "Take yourself off to work where you're needed."

Noah stiffened. "I'm not needed here?" He shook his head. "The doc said you need to rest that ankle. It might not be broken, but it's badly sprained." He gently threw a blanket over her, then left the sitting room.

Mary sighed. He was treating her like an invalid.

She glanced up to see him holding out a mug of tea. "Here you are. Now tell me you could have gotten that for yourself." She wanted to slap the smug grin off his face, but knew she never would. Noah was trying to help, as frustrating as she found her situation.

"If you make a list, Seth has offered to go to the mercantile for you." He studied her, no doubt waiting for Mary to argue. But how could she? They had little in the way of supplies and needed them. Otherwise she would never had ventured out on her own.

"If I must," she said, uncertainty in her voice. "Seth must have better things to do, surely?"

He raised his eyebrows. "It's what families do. You must know…" He suddenly stopped talking. No, she didn't know that. She'd never had a family that looked out for each other, and apparently Noah realized that. "Sorry."

He sunk down into the chair next to hers. "Seth offered, and I wasn't going to say no. He'll be here shortly to collect your list."

It was nice of him to offer, but she really wanted to go herself. As if reminding Mary of her predicament, her ankle began to throb and she winced.

"What can I do?" Noah asked, leaning toward her.

It was her turn to raise her eyebrows. "Get me a pencil and paper." She bit her lower lip. What would Noah say when he discovered her secret?

"For the pain, I meant." He retrieved the required items and handed them over.

"Are you sure Nelly's alright? You're not just saying that to make me feel better?" Noah had reassured her several times already, but Mary wasn't certain she believed him. It would be just like him to say that to make her feel better. "It's all my fault. I should have waited until you could go with me."

Noah reached across and held her hand. "For the tenth time – it was not your fault. It wasn't anyone's fault. Deer run across roads. They spook horses." His thumb stroking her palm was very reassuring and comforting. "It was nobody's fault. Nelly is fine except for a few little cuts, the buggy is already fixed, and you," He scratched his ear. "You will be fine in a couple of weeks as well."

She groaned. "I can't wait a couple of weeks." She tried to get up, but Noah held her back.

The more she tried, the closer he got, until they were almost face to face. He stared into her eyes. "You have to rest," he said quietly, and she nodded.

Mary's heart fluttered. He'd only ever been this close to her once before, and that was when he quickly kissed her for Seth's benefit. She stared into his eyes – they seemed to speak to her.

She lifted her hand and covered his cheek. Her hand shook and she swallowed back the emotion that surfaced. Noah had saved her life. If it wasn't for him, she wouldn't be here right now. Perhaps he did feel *something* for her. What that was, she had no idea.

He reached up and his hand covered hers, then he brought her hand to his lips and kissed it. A shudder went through her. Noah moved closer until their lips almost touched, and the breath caught in her throat.

She breathed in his fragrance, and reveled in his touch. He let go of her hand, and his arms slipped around her. Finally, Noah kissed her.

"Hello!"

"Damn it," Noah said under his breath. "Great timing," he said out loud to his brother.

Seth grinned. "Did I interrupt?" He winked at Mary. She felt the heat creep up her face at the embarrassment of it all.

"Mary hasn't had a chance to do the list yet."

Seth grinned again. "I can see that." He slapped Noah on the back. It was like there was some secret bond between them that Mary didn't understand.

"Can you do it, Noah," she asked hesitantly, and he studied her. He wrote down her requirements and he handed the list to his brother. "I was going to get some vegetable plants, but they can wait. It's not like I can do much now anyway." She stared down into her lap. All her plans had gone awry, and there wasn't a thing she could do about it.

"Tell me what you want and I'll see what I can find."

Mary explained what she wanted and Seth wrote it all down. "It would be nice to have fresh vegetables again," he said half joking.

Noah walked him out to the door, and if she didn't know better, Mary would have sworn he whispered something to his brother.

"Thanks Seth," he called as the buggy pulled away.

Noah snatched up his coffee and sat next to Mary again. He handed her the paper and pencil once more. "If you write down your recipe," he said, studying her. "I can make supper when Seth gets back."

Mary's heart thudded. He'd guessed. The last thing she wanted was for her husband to think she was even more of a fool than he already did.

"You know I can't," she said, staring down into her lap.

"Why didn't you tell me? It's not a crime. I could have helped you." He reached out and took her hand, bringing it close to his chest. She could feel his heart beating, and it soothed her.

She lifted her head to stare at him, and tears rolled down her cheeks. He wiped them away.

"Pa wouldn't let me attend school after Ma died," she said quietly. "I'd attend so few times before that…" Her voice broke and Mary couldn't continue. She turned her head, the shame of it eating at her.

"Mary," he said, his voice full of compassion.

She turned back to face him. "You guessed right," she said defiantly. "I can't read or write."

He gazed into her face for the longest of moments, then leaned in and kissed her gently. "I don't care about that," he said, cupping her face. "All I care about is that you are here with me. I can teach you, if that's what you want." He pulled her against him, and Mary reveled in their closeness, and in the bond they were finally beginning to share.

Chapter Seven

After handing her the bouquet of flowers he'd asked Seth to get for him, Noah made supper. It was only a small gesture, he'd told her, but to Mary it was huge. No one had ever bought flowers for her before. Never done anything nice for her. He really had no idea what it meant to her.

The gesture warmed her heart.

Supper wasn't quite the disaster she'd expected but it wasn't perfect either.

Mary insisted on peeling and dicing potatoes to go with the bacon, sausages, and eggs Noah was cooking. Just as well too as the eggs were rock hard, and the bacon burned to a crisp. Only the sausages survived. There was left over apple pie, which was a good thing as otherwise he would go hungry.

That wasn't really true. Since Seth had arrived home with all her requirements, there was plenty in the house to eat. As a thank you, she'd invited him and Jacob over for a meal one night, but not until her ankle was healed.

"I like your cooking far better," Noah told her.

She flashed him a shy smile. "I do too." He grinned at her and Mary let out the breath she'd been holding. She should know by now he didn't anger easily. In fact he seemed to like the easy banter they often shared. "My ankle isn't as bad as everyone is making out, so tomorrow you can go back to work."

He glared at her. "Ain't gonna happen," he said, then reached across the table for her hand. "Now the calving is done, I can take a few days off." She raised her eyebrows at him. "The cowpokes can look after the property. They've done it before."

She wasn't going to change his mind, that much was clear. Mary shrugged her shoulders – there were far more important things to argue over. This wasn't one of them.

Having to slow down because of an injured ankle was not amongst Mary's most favorite things to do. Noah was finally back at work, and she was almost pain free, even when she put pressure on her ankle and walked about.

Cinnamon stood outside the front porch waiting for Noah. She probably felt neglected after the number of days he'd stayed home to help. Mary stepped toward her, and the horse took a few steps back. "Take it slowly," Noah whispered. "She's still not used to you."

That was true. She'd had little interaction with Noah's horse, and he was the only person ever to ride her. "I'm going to miss you today," Mary said truthfully. She'd become accustomed to having her husband around, even if he was annoying by not letting her do things for herself.

His head shot up as he attached the saddlebags. "I'll miss you too," he said, then winked at her.

Was he only saying that? Mary found Noah hard to read at times. He seemed to keep his heart close to his chest, and didn't give away much.

He shoved his hat down hard on his head. "I really must go. It's been nice being home with you, but I can't stay home forever." He stared at her. "We'll continue our reading and writing lessons tonight."

She nodded. Mary had worked hard with Noah over the past days, and he said she was doing well. It didn't feel that way, but he was confident she would learn. Anger boiled up inside her at Pa for not letting her go to school.

Noah leaned forward and cupped her face, kissing her gently. Mary calmed down. It was as though he knew what she was thinking. "Don't be mad, Sweetheart," he said quietly, then caressed her cheek.

"How did you…?"

He winked at her. "I can read your moods now. What are you mad about anyhow?"

"Not what, who. I'm mad at Pa for not letting me go to school."

"You're going to learn better than going to school." He winked again then swung up onto his mount. Noah lifted the reins and clicked for Cinnamon to go. "I'll try not to be late." He turned and rode away.

Mary stared after him. They seemed to be getting closer, but would she and Noah ever have a real marriage? Right now, it didn't feel like it would ever happen.

She hobbled inside and cleaned the kitchen, then began to make the beds. What would it be like to sleep with Noah? That first night didn't count because she was asleep before he carried her to bed. No, she meant sleep with him in the real sense. As his actual wife, not them pretending to be a couple.

She lifted his pillow and breathed in the essence of Noah. How she longed to be his wife in every way.

Mary suddenly threw the pillow across the room with such force it thudded against the wall. That would never happen. She was only here to fulfil the obligations to his father's will. He gets the land, and she gets a safe place to live for a year. And then there was the money.

She shrugged. It meant little to her. Granted, when she arrived, even before she arrived, it was paramount. But now? Now it was of little consequence. Noah was the most important part of her life now.

How would she survive without him?

She didn't mean in a monetary sense, or even in regard to living somewhere safe. It seemed foolish, but even after just a few short months, Mary had become fond of Noah.

She shook her head. That wasn't true. It was so far from the truth it was almost laughable. She had come to love Noah, and couldn't imagine her life without him. A tear trickled down her face, and Mary swiped at her cheeks. She was being foolish. It was clear she was nothing but a convenience. A way to get his inheritance.

Noah wasn't interested in her, and had no feelings for her. He was likely counting the days until he could be rid of her.

She flopped down on the bed she'd just finished making. Life could be cruel, and this went beyond cruel. Short of throwing herself at her husband, Mary was doomed to a life of loneliness. What would happen to her once she was no longer part of Noah's life, she had no idea.

What she did know was she needed to start thinking about her future. She needed to plan her life after Noah – and that time was fast approaching.

Noah sat at the head of the table, Seth and Jacob sat either side.

Mary had worked endlessly throughout the day. It wasn't everyday you got to entertain family. She stopped and thought. She *did* have a family now, something she'd never had before. The table was dressed with Noah's best tablecloth and napkins, and she'd pulled out the best crockery she could find.

A freshly baked loaf of bread sat in the center of the table, and a plate of butter at each end. "Help yourselves," she said as Noah finished slicing the bread. "Supper won't be long."

A sparkling white dinner plate sat in front of each man, and another was there for Mary. The table was dressed as though it was Christmas.

“Going by the smell, we’re in for a treat,” Jacob said.

She pulled the oven door ajar and leaned in. “It sure does smell good,” Mary said. The heavy kitchen cloths she used on the oven dish stopped her from burning her hands. “I hope you all like lamb.” She turned to face them, the hot dish still in her hands, then placed it on the wooden board on the counter top.

“That looks amazing, Mary.” Noah came up behind her and took over, placing the lamb roast onto a plate where he could carve. As he carved, she dished out the vegetables and began to make the gravy, using the delicious juices from the meat.

“You are far too spoiled,” Seth told Noah. “I just about live on beans and bacon.”

Noah chuckled. “That was me before Mary came along. She’s an amazing cook, as you can see.”

Placing the gravy into two jugs, she placed one either end of the table. “Before we eat, I’d like to say something.” Mary’s heart thudded in her chest. It wasn’t often she had to make a speech, even if it was only to three people. When she glanced up, the three men were staring at her. Suddenly nervous, she sat down and placed her napkin on her lap.

"It's alright, Mary," Noah said. "We're all family here." As if he could sense how nervous she really was, he reached out and covered her hand. A shiver went through her.

She glanced at each man. They looked as tense as she felt. "I, I just wanted to thank you, each of you, for saving my life." She was met with silence.

Finally Jacob spoke. "There was never a question," he said quietly. "We look out for family, and you are a big part of ours now."

"That's right," Seth said.

She swallowed down the lump in her throat.

Then they all held hands and Noah said the blessing. "Thank you Lord for this abundance of food, and for sending Mary to us. We pray for the strength to grow as a family and face all challenges you send us. Amen."

Amen echoed around the table.

Mary's heart fluttered at his words.

Plates were filled, and light banter surrounded her. Warmth filled Mary as she finally felt as though she belonged.

It was such a joy to have real food to cook with. Not to mention surrounded by men who appreciated her cooking.

She had a blueberry pie cooling on the counter, along with a bread and butter pudding. Both favorites with Noah.

She sat back on her chair and glanced around the table. The three men talked about their various properties and what was going on with them. Suddenly Noah studied her. "I'm sorry. This discussion must be rather boring to you."

"I was rather enjoying it," she said. "Father never spoke at the table."

"Never?" Jacob asked.

"No, never." Except when he told her she was to marry Johnny Parsons. She preferred to forget that conversation. Mary waved her hands in front of her, dismissing the conversation. "How is your food?"

Seth grinned. "It is brilliant. I should pay you to cook for me every night. Better still, I could come here."

Noah glared at him. "It's never going to happen. Be grateful you were invited here tonight." Then he chuckled and Mary let go of the breath she'd been holding.

As the men finished their meal, she collected up the dishes and placed them in the sink. She cleared the table and prepared to serve dessert for her guests.

"Honestly," Jacob said. "This has to be the best meal I've ever eaten." Seth agreed. It made her feel warm inside.

Noah came up behind her and wrapped his arms around her. "You did a wonderful job," he said, then kissed her cheek. If only it was real instead of being for the benefit of his brothers. He lifted each of the desserts and placed them on the table. "Tuck in," he said.

Mary prepared the mugs for their coffee, then sat down.

She smiled at the groans of delight that echoed around the table. All in all, it was a successful night. It had been a thank you gesture from the start, and she felt sure it had done the trick.

"Tell me where you learned to cook like this," Seth asked.

"My mother. She was a terrific cook. At least she was before things got bad." Mary was horrified. She'd said too much and now everyone was staring at her.

Only her husband understood the context, and he reached out and gently squeezed her hand. "Well, wherever you learned to cook, we are all grateful for it. Aren't we boys?"

His brothers both nodded despite being confused. Suddenly they each took another mouthful of food.

"This really is delicious," Jacob said. "I'm not sure how you turn stale bread into such a delicacy, but you've done it," he said, reaching for another helping.

His comment made her smile. "The secret is in the jam," she said. Mary stood to make their coffees, then turned to face the three brothers. "You have no idea how much I appreciate you coming tonight," she said, her emotions beginning to bubble over. "Go into the sitting room when you are ready, and I'll bring your beverages."

She turned back before Noah spotted her tears. It was all far too much. The appreciation these three showed in one night, was far more than she'd received in a lifetime before.

How was she ever going to leave Broken Arrow Ranch? Worse still, how was she going to leave Noah – the only person who had ever meant anything to her.

Chapter Eight

"Last night was terrific," Noah said as he prepared to set out the next morning. "The food was delicious, and my brothers were really taken with you."

One moment she felt warm all over – she really liked Seth and Jacob – and the next she felt hollow. Not only would she have to leave Noah, whom she'd come to love, but also his brothers. They were decent people, all of them, and they'd made her feel like part of their family.

She swallowed down the lump in her throat. "It was a lovely evening," she told him quietly.

He reached out and put an arm around her shoulder. "I'm sure it helped sending them home with leftovers." He grinned down at her. "You made enough food to feed a small army."

Before Mary had a chance to answer or protest Noah pulled her to him and kissed her. Not gently on the cheek like an aunt or uncle might do, but directly on the lips.

His mouth came down over hers and her heart fluttered. She felt warm all over, and her arms slid up around him without her permission. She tipped her head back to give him more access to her, and she admonished herself. That was not the act of a lady. But then again, they were married, and this was what she'd been waiting for all these months. Wasn't it?

His hands slid into her hair, and she felt the pins come out one by one until her hair cascaded down her back. He lifted a piece of her hair and sniffed it, then suddenly he pushed her away, as if she was forbidden fruit, and touching her might kill him. She stared up into his face. She felt hurt, pained at the fact he didn't want her after all, so his next words took her by surprise.

"I want you, Mary," he said, his voice husky. "Like I've never wanted anyone before." Without warning, he slipped his strong arms underneath her and carried her to the bedroom. His bedroom. She didn't complain, and soon she was Noah's wife in every sense of the word.

When she awoke, Noah was gone. He'd been so gentle with her, caring and loving.

Was this what it would be like to be Noah's wife? For the first time in her life, it felt as though someone cared for her. Really cared for her, not just because she could clean house and cook, but it was as though she meant something to him.

Which was crazy because she'd been here all this time and it was only now that he'd wanted to... Of course men had longings, and their wives need to fulfil those longings. She was surprised he'd waited so long.

She suddenly sat up in bed, her heart pounding. How long had she laid about like a lady of leisure? She needed to prepare supper, not to mention organize the household chores. The last thing she wanted was for him to think of her as lazy. Just because they'd…she swallowed…it didn't mean she got to laze around and do nothing.

Mary stood, then straightened the bed, embarrassed at the thoughts of what had occurred in that bed a short time ago. She had to get it through her head she was a true married woman now, and this is what men expected of their wives. She suddenly realized she stood naked. Noah had slowly removed every item of clothing from her body, and then removed his own. At first she was shocked to see him undressed. She'd never seen a naked man before.

Well, that wasn't quite true. She felt the heat creep up her face at the memory of the first time she'd seen him – that day in the bathtub. But she'd averted her eyes as quickly as she possibly could.

But he really was beautiful to look at, and Mary decided she would never tire of seeing him that way. Then it hit her, this was meant to be a marriage of convenience. Or was *she* a convenience to him?

Was that how it would be from now on – that Noah would use her body when it was convenient to him?

She felt hollow and wasn't sure what she should do now. She couldn't leave, she'd signed the contract and agreed to stay for one whole year. There was far too much time left on that contract.

One thing she did know – it was going to be a very long year. It seemed silly, but after only a matter of months, she felt enamored to the man. No, that wasn't true. Mary was deeply in love with him.

The sun was shining, the air was warm, and Mary decided to work in the garden. She'd recently planted all the vegetables Seth had obtained for her, but there was still a lot to do. The garden beds had been overgrown with weeds, and it had proven a lot of work to be rid of them.

The chickens had a great curiosity toward those plants too, and it was all Mary could do to keep them away. "Shoo! Shoo!" she told them as she stood up to chase them away. She loved the eggs they produced, but had never been fond of chickens. Especially the ones that pecked.

Nor did she like roosters. She'd been harassed by more than one rooster over the years. She shivered. They really did bother her.

She collected up the eggs and took them inside. Noah had stopped selling the eggs to the mercantile. He didn't need the money, and most of the time Mary used them up with her baking. If there was one thing she knew about Noah, it was that he loved food. In particular, he loved her food. If she were truthful, she loved to cook for him. With all the supplies at her fingertips, Mary got so much joy from baking.

She spent the time to bake for him, and he spent the time teaching her to read and write. It was slow going, but she was coming along nicely. At least that's what Noah told her, so she had to believe it.

Tonight they would have a beef stew with dumplings for supper. Noah's favorite.

With supper organized, and the laundry on the line, it was time for a break. Mary pulled a mug down from the cupboard. It was then she heard the commotion out front. The chickens were making quite a racket, and she ran to the front door.

“For goodness sakes, go away,” Seth was saying, chasing the chickens away with his hat. He glanced up at her, frowning. “How do you stand the horrible creatures?”

She couldn’t help but smile. “I don’t like them either,” she said. “But I need their eggs. Occasionally one will lose their head.”

He appeared shocked at her words and studied her. “Seriously?”

Mary’s smile disappeared. “Of course. Sometimes when you have no food to eat, you have to sacrifice future eggs. It’s the way of the world.” She shrugged her shoulders, then held the door open for him. “Noah’s not here.” She glanced back over her shoulder at him, curious as to why he was here.

Seth followed her into the kitchen and slumped down at the table. “I was in the area, and longed for a coffee,” he said. “I didn’t think you’d mind.” He suddenly grinned.

Mary chuckled. It wasn’t her coffee he’d come for, but her baking. “I just happen to have an orange cake. Freshly baked yesterday.” She didn’t bother to ask if he’d like some – she already knew the answer.

She pulled the tin down from the overhead cupboard and the cake on the wooden board. She placed a plate laden with sliced cake in front of Seth. He reached over and took a bite. "This is delicious," he told her. "If you ever decide you no longer want Noah, I'm your man." He grinned cheekily and Mary knew he was joking.

She stared at him over the top of her mug. "You should get yourself a wife. Make sure she can bake first."

He almost spat his coffee out, then became suddenly serious. "I do have to find a wife, like Noah did. At least I have more time, but still, it has to happen eventually."

Mary swallowed. Another woman would be put in the same situation as her. "Make sure you love her, Seth." She blinked rapidly, trying to force her tears away.

He stared at her curiously. "Noah loves you."

She was too overcome with emotion to speak, and shook her head instead.

"Mary," he said, reaching across to cover her hand. It was big like Noah's and every bit as work roughened. "Noah loves you. It is very plain to everyone who sees the two of you together."

She tried to swallow down the lump in her throat. "The truth is," she said quietly. "Noah only tolerates me because of the will. If he didn't have to keep me here because of the contract, he would have rid himself of me by now." Tears rolled down her cheeks, she couldn't stop the flow.

Seth stared at her. "You can't mean that. Noah loves you, he does." Seth stepped toward her, and pulled Mary to him. His arms were comforting, but she knew she shouldn't allow herself to be held by a man who was not her husband. What if Noah came home? She didn't want to be the cause of a rift between the brothers.

His fingers under her chin forced Mary to look up at him. It was almost like staring at Noah. "Do you love him, Mary?" He looked sad, as though he really cared for her. "Do you want to be Noah's wife?"

Her voice barely audible, she answered him. "I do."

"Then…"

"What are you doing holding my wife?" The door slammed and Noah stormed in. Mary's heart pounded and her head hurt.

"It's not what you think," Mary told him.

He dragged his wife from Seth's arms. "Are you alright?" He stared down into her face. "You've been crying. What did you do to her, Seth?" Noah stiffened and glared at his brother.

"It's not what *I* did," Seth said, extending himself to his full height, which was taller than Noah. "It's what *you* didn't do." He turned to Mary. "Thanks for the coffee and cake. Sort it out – for both your sakes, sort it out." He snatched up his hat from the rack at the door, and was gone before Mary could say another word.

Noah held her away and stared at her. "Did Seth hurt you?"

She shoved herself away from him. "Of course not. That's what *you* did."

Noah looked confused. "What I did? I don't understand."

"I can't do it, Noah. I can't continue to be your wife." She took a long, shuddering breath. Her husband studied her. He truly didn't understand what was going on. "I know when I'm not wanted, so I'll pack my things and go." His face was devoid of all color.

"I don't understand," he whispered. "I know I don't say it enough, but I love you, Mary. Don't leave me." She'd never seen him look so utterly devastated.

She stared at the floor. "You've never said it, so how do I know you're not just saying that?"

He reached out and pulled her against him. "I do love you, Mary. I have from that first day."

Did he? Did he really, or was he only trying to appease her? "You don't act like it," she snapped. "All these months, and you only recently took me to your bed."

"I don't force women," he said, staring down into her face. "You didn't seem to be willing, so I left you alone." His thumb swiped at her tears. "Please don't cry. You're breaking my heart. I don't want you to leave either. I want you to stay."

"Until the contract is up," she whispered.

He frowned down at her. "No…I want you here forever. I love you too much to lose you. We were meant to be together."

Mary snuggled into her husband's chest. "I love you too," she said quietly. "I think I have from that first moment you helped me on the train platform."

"What a couple of dills we are," he said gently. "We are both too silly for our own good."

He slid his hand underneath her and carried Mary to their bedroom.

Mary sat on the ground tending to her vegetable patch. The chickens were annoying her as usual, and she stood, then chased them away.

Her basket was filled with carrots, potatoes, corn, and beans. "These will be lovely for supper," she told Noah as she walked into the kitchen.

Seth and Jacob were coming over, and they were having a lovely family dinner. Noah and Seth had made up long ago – in fact, Noah had thanked his brother for ensuring everything came out in the open.

She scraped the potatoes and added them to a pot, then did the same for the carrots. By the time these were ready, the roast chicken would be perfectly cooked. Noah came up behind her and wrapped her in his loving arms, then kissed her neck. So much had changed after that day Seth had unexpectedly visited.

Mary was certain it must have been a message from God.

She heard the horses before anything else, and turned to her husband. "At least one of our guests are here," she told him.

"They're not guests," he said, chuckling. "It's only my brothers." Noah turned to go outside while the brothers tended to their horses in the barn.

"They're early." They were always early. Usually trying to get cake before supper. It made her laugh.

Mary made her way to the sitting room. She had been busy most of the day and now that supper was under control, she needed to rest. She sat on one of the comfortable chairs, closed her eyes and was quickly asleep. The next thing she knew, Noah was standing over her.

"Do you need to lay down for awhile?" he asked, concern on his face.

She shook her head. "I'm fine." She reached for his hand. "Feel this," she said, staring into his amazed face. "It won't be long, and we'll get to meet our baby."

"I still can't believe I was so lucky to find you," he whispered. "I love you more than you'll ever know."

Tears filled Mary's eyes. Her faith in God was restored that day back in Angel's Pass when two virtual strangers made her an offer that would save her life.

She finally had a family who loved and appreciated her. When Seth and Jacob eventually married, she would get the sisters she never had.

She loved it here on Broken Arrow Ranch, and knew she would never leave.

From the Author

Thank you so much for reading my book – I hope you enjoyed it.

I would greatly appreciate you leaving a review where you purchased, even if it is only a one-liner. It helps to have my books more visible!

Look out for the other books in the Brides of Broken Arrow series.

About the Author

Multi-published, award-winning and bestselling author, Cheryl Wright, former secretary, debt collector, account manager, writing coach, and shopping tour hostess, loves reading.

She writes both historical and contemporary western romance, as well as romantic suspense.

She lives in Melbourne, Australia, and is married with two adult children and has six grandchildren. When she's not writing, she can be found in her craft room making greeting cards.

Links:

Website: *http://www.cheryl-wright.com/*

Blog: *http://romance-authors.com/*

Facebook Reader Group:
https://www.facebook.com/groups/cherylwrightaut hor/

Join My Newsletter:

https://cheryl-wright.com/newsletter/

CPSIA information can be obtained
at www.ICGtesting.com
Printed in the USA
LVHW040354211222
735681LV00009B/517